The Wood

Written by Shaun Brennan   Illustrated by Margaux Meganck

Thank you to our
Storytellers:

Topher Smith, Dan Pearson, Jenna Silva, Terry Rossiter, Chiron Herweg, Jim and Christie O'Brien, Sean Ferrin, Gordie d'Avignon, Catherine Butler, James Coyle, Michael Green, Michael and Lisa Brennan, Robert Middlebrooks, Leah Cooper, Jason Carey, Amanda Lehman, Machael Badger, K. Woods, Sterling Hundley, Joe Jorgenson, Beth Penny, Doug Curry, Manish Dalmia, Lee Halverson, Cheryl Brennan, Robert Meganck, Corky Keck, Naomi Leovao-Carpel, Rodney and Andi Murray, Patricio Harrington, Dakota Lindsey, Sarah Wiebenson, Patricia Pascone, Miranda Steed, Ronald A. Spencer, Derek Bigelow, Meghan Wulff, Ben Graeff, Hannah Kingrey, Yvonne and Jason Stephens, Jack Donovan, Jo Monterosso, Christopher Green, Kavi Pandey, Aron Williams, Peggy Harrison, Layna George, Ryan Ogborn, Martha Awdziewicz, Brian Jacobson, Katie McDonald, Donne Egle, Kendra Read, Mickey W ston, Micheal Lea, Jill Braman, Kyle Hurst, Jason Beck, Justin House, Elise Mclellan, Marilyn Welniak, Eric von Paternos, Ellen C. Miller, Colleen Vedder, Ally Hodges, Beth Hoover, Pete Lawton, Brian Bing, Beki Riley, Tim Mobeck, Judith Anderson, Eric Yatskowitz, Joan Curry, Lindsey Donavan, Matthew Tooley, Mike Campbell, Seano and Vishnu, Brad Hinkel, Julie Byers, Ian Cavalier, Kristen Mitchell, Kristen Morgan-May, Logan Gianni, Christopher Nichols, Ruben Davila, Ryan Hicks, Simon Tucker, Courtney Sullivan, Blair Maschal, Trevor Yates, Maree Wellings, Kyle Baxley, John Eckstein, Duane Rice, Alex Weyermann, Eric Damon Walters, Chris Lincoln, Kevin and Lauren Brennan, Vicki Brennan, Sara F. Hoffman, Mariann and Bobby Waide, Dave and Jen Mondoux, Rick Tabor, Ryan Dubuc, Ken Nagasako, Noah Ullmann, Raga Teiaka Veratau, Janusz Kruszewski, Jeremy Lux, Judy Butler, Jason Creech, Sarah Worman, Stuart Lofthouse, Gesa Ziggert, Jonty Levine, Stacy Macleod, Nicholas Bevan, Katherine Bolding, Joseph Cortese, Rebecca Mutch, Samuel Adams Greene, Charles Meier, Ruthie Kelly, Rhett Sellers, Gemma Johnson, Caroline Leu, Justin Kim, James and Sandra Brennan.

To Jim and Sandy Brennan, for teaching me that pursuit of mystery and a sense of wonder does not require superstition and fear.

One day a poor Woodsman went
to the forest to cut down a tree.

He needed wood to make into furniture and carvings to feed himself and his son. Even though he was a skilled craftsman, his family rarely had any money because his son was often very sick, and the medicine was very expensive.

This time the Woodsman sought to earn a great deal of money, perhaps enough for the rest of his and his son's days. He had heard that one of the fabled Heart Trees was located in the forest to the east. Heart Trees are extremely rare, and their wood is very expensive.

So the Woodsman hoped that with his skill as a carver, he could make an item of inestimable value.

He traveled through the forest, passing through the Glowing Glen and around Looking Glass Lake. He made his way down through the Valley of Stars, past the Luminous River, and there at last he found the tree. It was nestled in a nameless glade in the crook of the Cloud Cap Mountains. He stood before the tree and looked it over for a time.

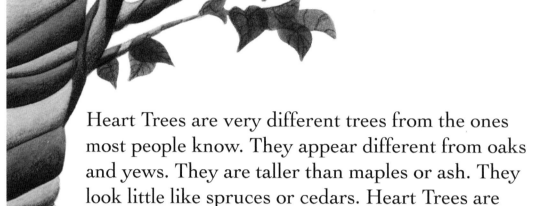

Heart Trees are very different trees from the ones most people know. They appear different from oaks and yews. They are taller than maples or ash. They look little like spruces or cedars. Heart Trees are very peculiar trees, for you see, they have no bark.

Their wood is exposed except for a thin sheen of sap, which makes them look like a polished table. In fact, Heart Trees always appear to be carved, even as they grow. Their wood is smooth and fine-grained. The grain appears as two alternating layers, one nearly blood red, and the other pale beige.

Their leaves are red with purple veins that splay in all directions. And in the middle of the trunk of every Heart Tree is a knot that all agree looks quite a bit like a heart. It is from this knot that the Heart Tree draws its name.

As the Woodsman finished his inspection of the tree, he came to rest his hand upon it. The wood felt warm and strangely soft to the touch. Running his hand over the surface of the wood, he looked up through the canopy of the Heart Tree at the sun.

It seemed to him that the leaves swayed without regard to wind. Their movement seemed measured and even, like a person's breath. Moving slowly away from the tree, the Woodsman sat down and began removing his ax, hatchet, and saw from his bundle.

When he leaned the axe against the tree, the leaves began to quiver. Puzzled, the Woodsman stood up, placing his hand on the tree as he did so. When his hand touched the tree, strange images flooded his mind.

He saw a beautiful woman, tall and graceful, with blooms and leaves woven in her hair. She stood before him, wearing a gown of intertwined vines and multicolored leaves. Her eyes were most captivating, and they held his gaze.

"I am a Dryad," the woman announced. "I live within this Heart Tree, and I will perish if you cut it down! I have lived in this forest for many centuries, watching the world and the animals within it. I have harmed no one, and I have brought shade, shelter, and food to many a creature. Would you kill such a being?"

The Woodsman was taken aback. "Of course not! I was unaware that this Heart Tree contained a Dryad. Please accept my apologies. I will seek out another Heart Tree, one without such a fine creature within it. Could you tell me where I might find one?"

She looked at him sadly. "I cannot do that, for you see, all Heart Trees have a Dryad or some other fey creature within them. The trees grow from the bodies of the fey when they die, and house their souls till the end of days."

The Dryad looked with compassion upon the Woodsman standing there before her in his plain clothes, his hat clutched plaintively in his hands. "Perhaps there is something else we could do. If you were careful, and are as skilled as you imply, then you could carve my wood without cutting down or harming me. If you were to carefully carve and shape the trunk of my tree into something beautiful, would it be of value?"

The Woodsman perked up at this. "I...I think so.

I have heard of museums where people pay money to look at fine works of art. This could be a natural museum! And do not worry, I shall be very careful."

"Then that we shall do. You may begin carving me at once. Please be careful, for I will not be able to talk with you again for many years. It is difficult for me to communicate with a creature such as you. You will hear only the rustling of my leaves, and see the swaying of my branches."

"I have only my felling tools, I will need to get my carving implements, so I must return in a few days. Do not worry, I will be very careful, Dryad."

"Very well, I will see you in a few days..." she said, as she faded away.

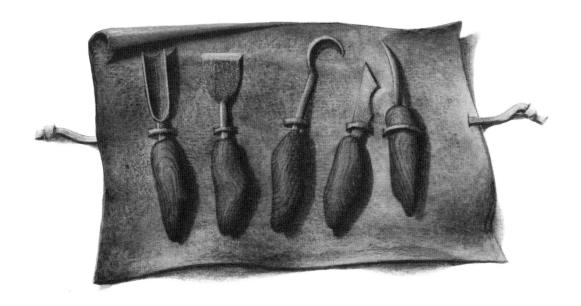

The Woodsman found himself alone in the glade again, with his hand still against the tree. Shaking his head, he packed away his tools and hurried home.

Making his way home, the Woodsman considered what he would carve. He thought of the beautiful birds and fearsome bears and stately mountain cats he had seen in the forest. They all seemed inappropriate to carve on such a tree.

So he thought instead of the boisterously colored wildflowers and verdant glades and elegant vines he had passed along his journeys. Yet they too seemed wrong to put on such a tree.

What lesser image could one carve on such a natural thing of beauty? Arriving at his cottage at the edge of the forest, the Woodsman still did not have his answer.

The Woodsman entered his cottage and found the Son sitting in his usual chair by the window, reading in the sunlight. The Son looked up from his book. "Back so soon? Did you get the Heart Tree wood already?"

"No," the Woodsman replied. "The Heart Tree contains a Dryad, a beautiful fey creature, and I cannot cut the tree down without killing her."

"That is terrible! I am glad you did not cut down the tree, but what will you do instead?"

"The Dryad and I discussed it, and she said it would be alright if I carved her wood into something beautiful and set it up as a work of art for people to pay to see. Like in a museum." answered the Woodsman.

"That's a wonderful idea! With your beautiful carving and the uniqueness of the Heart Tree, people will come from miles around!"

"I suppose so," responded the Woodsman.

"Why are you so glum?" asked the Son. "It seems that everything will work out after all."

"Perhaps. It's just that I cannot figure out what to carve on such a lovely tree. I have never seen its equal. Carving something less would feel like soiling the wood. And when the Dryad herself appeared in my mind, she appeared as a woman with all the beauty of nature."

"I see. Perhaps you could carve the Dryad's visage into the Heart Tree itself?"

The Woodsman's eyes went wide. "That is the perfect thing. That is exactly what I will do!"

"I would like to go with you to see the Heart Tree and watch you carve," said the Son.

"Go with me? But you are not well."

"Yes, I would like to go. You have always taken good care of me, but it has been years since I have been outside this house. Besides, this carving will take a long time, and it will go faster if you do not have to keep returning here to care for me."

"That is true, it will take a long time. I worry for you, though, and I wish for you to be happy."

"I know you do, but this will make me the happiest of all—to be with you, and to see the Heart Tree."

"Very well, then, tomorrow we will set off," said the Woodsman.

The two ventured out the next morning, taking food and water enough for many a day.

The pair made their way slowly so as to not to tax the Son's strength too much.

When they arrived at the glade and stood before the tree, the Son saw framed within the Heart Tree a glowing woman beautiful to behold, with leaves and flowers woven into her hair. She looked at him with acorn-brown eyes that were streaked with green, blue, and purple.

He stood enraptured, gazing at her.

"Dryad, I do not know if you can hear me, but I have returned," the Woodsman said. "I have also brought with me my—what is it, Son?"

"I—I can see her. I can see the Dryad. You were right, she is a woman with all the beauty of nature."

"You can?" asked the Woodsman, "The Dryad said she can only speak and be seen every few years."

"I do not understand it, but I can see her all the same: rosy cheeks, soft brown skin, warm smile, and delicate hands," the Son said. The Dryad blushed at his words.

"That is her. You must describe her while I work."

While the Woodsman worked, the Dryad began to sing for them with the rustling of her leaves and the sighing of gusts of the wind.

The Son and the Woodsman sat and listened to the beautiful song. The Son was surprised to find he could understand the words. When she had finished, he asked the name of the song.

The Dryad said, "'Springtime in the Meadow.'"

"That's a lovely name for a lovely song," said the Son.

"You can hear me?" the Dryad asked, surprised.

"I can. You have a melodic voice—if I may say so," the Son said bashfully.

"You are the first person to hear my words without my having to bring them into the Fey, as I did with the Woodsman. And... thank you. You are very kind to say so."

At that point, the Woodsman came over, having overheard half of the conversation.

"You are able to hear the Dryad as well as see her?" he asked the Son.

"I can. And I can speak to her too."

"Have I hurt her? With the carving, I mean."

"He has not," said the Dryad.

"She says you have not hurt her," the boy told his father. "I can translate what she says for you, if you wish."

"I do, and thank you. What did she say was the name of the song?"

"'Springtime in the Meadow.'"

"Ah. That is a lovely name," said the Woodsman.

From then on, whenever the Dryad and the Woodsman needed to speak, the Son would relay her words.

So the days passed, the Son describing the Dryad, the Woodsman carving, and the Dryad singing.

When the Woodsman and the Son were hungry, the Dryad would tell them of trees or bushes with ripe fruit, or of rabbit burrows, or where mushrooms could be found.

Sometimes they would all sit around conversing, discussing the change of the seasons and the passage of life.

As time went on, the Woodsman grew more content with just listening. He would sit with his back against an oak, watching and listening to the Son and the Dryad talk, a warm smile on his face.

The Son and the Dryad spoke of many things, but the conversation would always return to how they both saw the world from a solitary viewpoint.

The Son had always been confined to the house he shared with the Woodsman. Indeed this was the first time he had ever been outdoors for this long. His view of the world had always come through one of the cottage's four windows.

He could never touch the things he saw, but he often wrote stories about them—oaks that had been there since time immemorial, raccoons with a dozen kits to feed, great hawks who ruled over the forest from their lofty perches.

The Dryad found his stories very entertaining, because for as long as she could remember, she had seen the world the same way. She had seen great oaks grow from acorns, stretch toward the sky, and finally fall back to the earth hundreds of years later. She had spied the crafty raccoon out with her kits at night, searching for fallen fruit.

She had watched innumerable hawks fly overhead and occasionally make nests in her branches. It made her laugh to imagine a mortal thinking this way.

"Can you not just walk outdoors?" the Dryad had asked.

"I cannot, for I am too sick to do so. I have been sick my entire life. So I have never really been outside before this."

"That is sad. I could not imagine not feeling the sun on my leaves, or the wind in my branches, or my roots in the soil."

"Well, I do not know how it feels for leaves, branches, and roots. But I have enjoyed feeling the sun on my face, the wind in my hair, and the soil between my toes." said the Son as he wiggled his toes in the turf.

"Hee hee. I think I would enjoy wiggling my roots, if I could," said the Dryad. "Do you know how it is that you are able to hear me? None other can."

"I do not know, Dryad. I have often been able to perceive things others could not. I knew our cat was with kittens before anyone else did, and I could see that the owl that lived in the maple near our house would die days before he did."

"I see. And that is why you are able to see me as well?"

"I think so," the boy said. "I must admit that the outside world is quite strange, but I'm glad there is someone like you out here. And that I was able to meet you."

"Thank you," said the Dryad. "And thank you for describing me as you have. During my idle time, I have often pictured myself as a human, and your descriptions are very flattering."

"You are welcome," replied the Son shyly. "You are very beautiful, and I have only done my best to describe what my eyes see."

"How did you come to be a Heart Tree?" the Son asked of the Dryad.

"When a Fey creature dies, if it is buried in the bole of a fallen oak with a pinecone, a walnut, and a sprig of laurel wrapped in a Heart Tree leaf, then a Heart Tree will grow there. The Fey creature's memories and soul will enter the Heart Tree, and they will become one."

"The memories do not last for long, though, at least not strongly. It is hard to remember legs and feet when you have a trunk and roots. Arms and hands seem strange when you have branches and leaves. Some things stay forever, but most memories fade into a haze of images."

"That is sad," said the Son, "that you cannot remember your past life."

"It is not too bad. The days are filled with new experiences, and one should not live only in memory, especially if one is a tree, for there are many hours spent in contemplation, and one can lose track of the present."

"That is true," replied the Son. "I hadn't thought of that. I think that I should like to be a Heart Tree, if ever I could."

The final stage of the carving was very time-consuming and delicate.

The Woodsman had to stop frequently to discuss with the Son what to carve, asking about minute details and subtle points.

"Her eyes are hazel and brown, they also turn slightly upwards," the Son would say, or, "Her hair falls over her shoulder like a winding stream."

The Woodsman and the Son spent long periods discussing these things to ensure they were just right. This became more difficult when the Son's condition began to worsen.

Soon, even just sitting and describing the Dryad took its toll on the Son, and they had to take more frequent breaks. The Woodsman began to despair of finishing the carving.

As they drew to the completion of the carving, the Son grew weaker, and then weaker still. Finally the Woodsman made a small cot for the Son so that he could lie right next to where the Woodsman was working, whispering directions and descriptions.

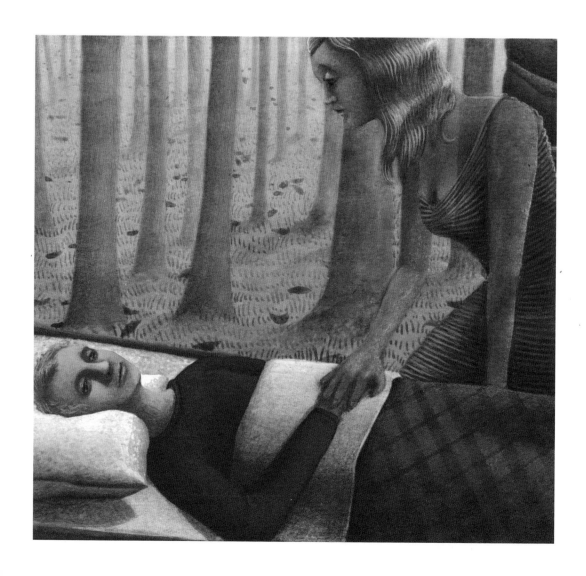

During the last few days, the father and Son's conversations ceased as well, as the boy became too weak to talk. Before he lost his ability to speak, he asked his father to lean him against the Heart Tree whenever possible.

It seemed he could still converse with the Dryad if he actually touched her.

The Woodsman soon simply left the Son leaning against the tree, for by now he knew what to carve. The Son had described the Dryad so often, the Woodsman knew her as if he could always see her.

When the Woodsman finished, he lifted the Son and stood him in front of the Dryad. The Son smiled and said, "Yes, Father, that is her. Thank you, and thank you for bringing me here."

"You are welcome, Son, and thank you for helping me with this." And with that, the Son died.

The Woodsman buried the Son in the bole of a fallen oak with a pinecone, a walnut, and a sprig of laurel wrapped in a Heart Tree leaf.

A tree grew from him upon his burial, quickly reaching a height of twenty feet. As it grew, its branches and roots intertwined with those of the Dryad's tree.

A year later, the Woodsman returned. He began carving the Son's tree. He did all the work without ever opening his eyes, carving his son as he saw him in his mind: hale, sound of body, a wise man of middle years with a compassionate countenance.

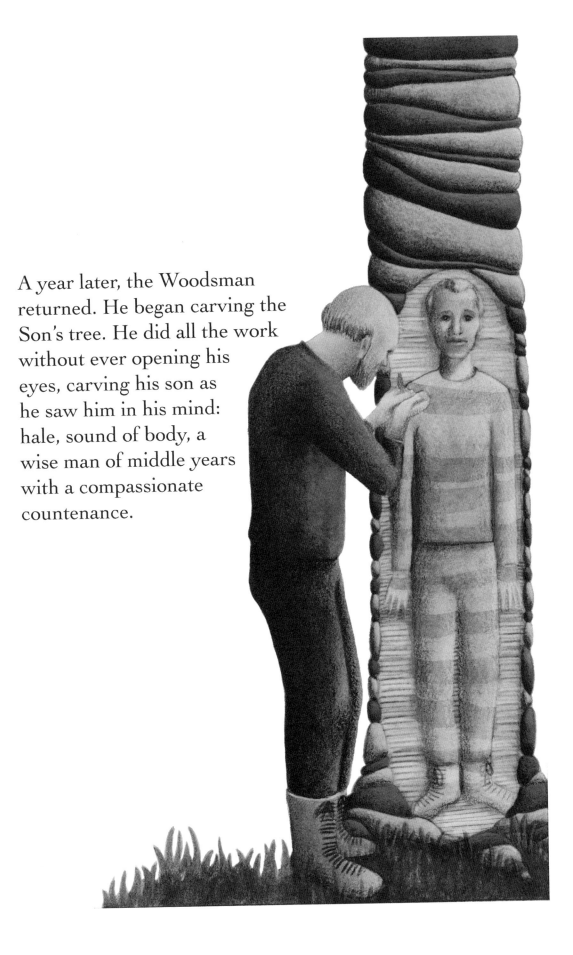

The two trees stand there still;

the Lovers forever arm in arm.

The End

About the author: **Shaun Brennan** grew up in Bloomfield Hills, Michigan. He spent his younger years climbing through woods, looking for frogs and tree spirits. He found a lot more of the former than the latter, though the latter have had a greater effect. He has spent a lot of years working on things that aren't writing and is happy to have completed his first book. Current whereabouts are Earth, Sol System, Local Interstellar Cloud, Local Bubble, Orion–Cygnus Arm, Milky Way Galaxy.

About the illustrator: **Margaux Meganck** lives and works in her Portland, Oregon home. She loves drinking tea, drawing, painting, and playing fun games with her friends. You can see more of her work at margauxmeganck.com or follow her illustration blog at margauxmeganck.blogspot.com.

Made in the USA
Charleston, SC
30 May 2013